MUSEUM MYSTERIES

Museum Mysteries is published by Stone Arch Books
A Capstone Imprint
1710 Roe Crest Drive
North Mankato, MN 56003
www.capstoneyoungreaders.com

Text and illustrations © 2015 Stone Arch Books

Library of Congress Cataloging-in-Publication Data
Brezenoff, Steven, author.
  The case of the missing museum archives / by Steve Brezenoff ; illustrated by Lisa K. Weber.
       pages cm. -- (Museum mysteries)
Summary: When the plans for the Bat-Wing, a historical aircraft, disappear from the Capitol City Air and Space Museum, eleven-year-old Amal Farah's father is blamed, and it is up to the four young friends to solve the mystery and save her father's job.
ISBN 978-1-4342-9688-7 (library binding) -- ISBN 978-1-4342-9692-4 (pbk.) -- ISBN 978-1-4965-0197-4 (ebook PDF) -- ISBN 978-1-4965-2191-0 (reflowable epub)
1. Astronautical museums--Juvenile fiction. 2. Theft from museums--Juvenile fiction. 3. Criminal investigation--Juvenile fiction. 4. Detective and mystery stories. 5. Best friends--Juvenile fiction. [1. Mystery and detective stories. 2. Astronautical museums--Fiction. 3. Museums--Fiction. 4. Stealing--Fiction. 5. Criminal investigation--Fiction. 6. Best friends--Fiction. 7. Friendship--Fiction. 8. Arab Americans--Fiction.] I. Weber, Lisa K., illustrator. II. Title.
PZ7.M47833755 Cam 2015
813.6--dc23
                                                                    2014025996

Designer: K. Carlson
Editor: A. Deering
Production Specialist: G. Bentdahl

Photo Credits: Shutterstock (vector images, backgrounds, paper textures); NASA (ISS); Library of Congress Prints and Photographs Division (Wright brothers flight)

Printed in China
092014   008472RRDS15

The Case of the
MISSING MUSEUM
ARCHIVES

By Steve Brezenoff
Illustrated by Lisa K. Weber

STONE ARCH BOOKS
a capstone imprint

Fact Sheet:
German "Bat-Wing" Plane

Physical Description: WWII; twin-jet engines; delta shape; steel fuselage with wood coverage

Country of Origin: Germany

Manufacturer: Horten, Reimar and Walter

Wingspan: 16.8 m (55.4 ft)

Length: 7.47 m (24.6 ft)

Height: 2.81 m (9.3 ft)

Weights: 5,067 kg (11,198 lb)

Engines: (2) Junkers-Jumo 004 B-2 turbojet

Notes: Considered the first stealth plane. Test flights had multiple crashes. Design abandoned.

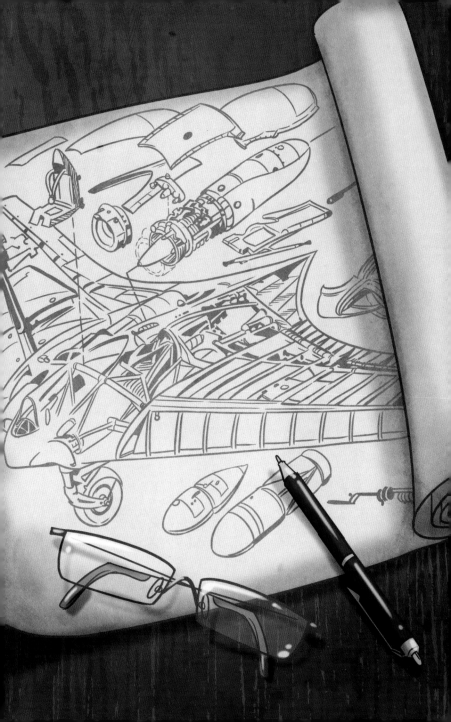

Amal Farah

Raining Sam

Wilson Kipper

Clementine Wim

Capitol City Sleuths

Amal Farah
Age: 11
Favorite Museum: Air and Space Museum
Interests: astronomy, space travel, and
building models of space ships

Raining Sam
Age: 12
Favorite Museum: American History Museum
Interests: Ojibwe history, culture, and
traditions, American history – good and bad

Clementine Wim
Age: 13
Favorite Museum: Art Museum
Interests: painting, sculpting with clay, and
anything colorful

Wilson Kipper
Age: 10
Favorite Museum: Natural History Museum
Interests: dinosaurs (especially pterosaurs
and herbivores), and building dinosaur models

TABLE OF

CONTENTS

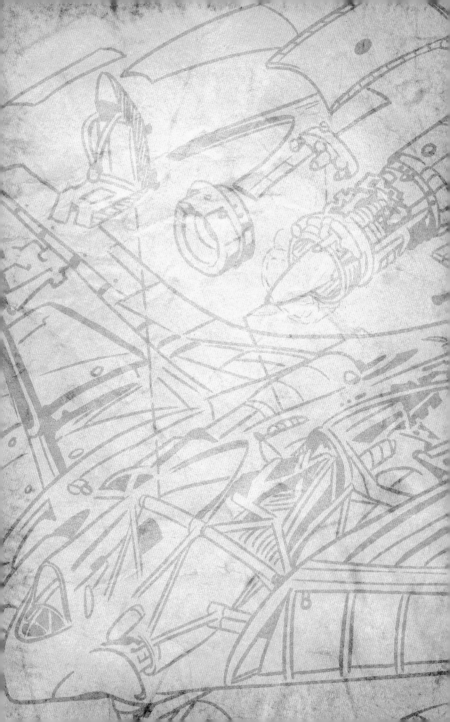

CHAPTER 1
Running Late

Eleven-year-old Amal Farah lay on the floor of her bedroom on her back. Even though it was just after breakfast and the sun was shining brightly outside, Amal gazed up at the stars and planets — a solar system mobile and glow-in-the-dark stars on her bedroom ceiling.

"Amal?" said a voice near her head. "Hello? Earth to Amal?" It was Raining Sam, one of her best friends, on the phone. She'd totally zoned out while talking.

Amal would never forget the first time she'd heard Raining's name. She and her father, Dr. Ahmed Farah, had just moved to Capitol City because he'd gotten a new job at the Air and Space Museum. Raining Sam had been one of the first kids she'd met when they arrived.

Raining's mother had just started at the American History Museum, which was run by the same non-profit organization as the Air and Space Museum. He'd accompanied his mother to the museum's orientation, just like Amal had accompanied her father.

During dinner that night, Amal had laughed and said, "Raining Sam? Is that a name or a weather report?"

She'd meant it as a joke, but her father hadn't been amused. "A lot of people you meet in Capitol City might think our Somali names are pretty funny too," he'd said with a pointed look.

Amal knew just what he meant. That had been only a few weeks ago. Since then, Amal and Raining had become close friends. She'd quickly learned that Raining knew almost nothing about astronomy, her favorite subject, but he was equally interested in Ojibwe — the name of his tribe of indigenous people.

And Amal hadn't laughed at his name even one more time.

"Sorry," she apologized. "I called to see if you want to come with me to the Air and Space Museum today. Dad's going to let me hang there today while he's working."

Raining didn't answer. Instead, he moved the phone away from his mouth and shouted, "Mom! Can I hang out with Amal today at the Air and Space?" A moment later he said into the phone, "She says I can."

"Great!" Amal replied happily. "We'll pick you up. And don't worry about packing lunch. Dad will get us free food in the cafeteria."

"Hot dogs?" Raining asked.

"Whatever you want, I guess," Amal said. "See you soon."

Amal jumped to her feet, jammed her phone into the pocket of her jeans, and grabbed her favorite headscarf off the chair at her desk.

Her dad was always telling her she needed to do a better job of keeping her scarves better organized so they wouldn't always be wrinkled or lost. But what was the point? This one — dark blue with a pattern of gold stars — was the only one she ever wanted to wear anyway.

"I'm ready, Dad," Amal said as she hurried down the stairs.

Her father stood at the front door tapping his foot. His museum ID badge dangled from his shirt pocket. "Finally," he said impatiently. "Hurry up and get in the car. We'll be late!"

"We have to pick up Raining on the way," Amal said quickly as she zipped through the open front door and flashed a grin at her dad. "Hurry, hurry!"

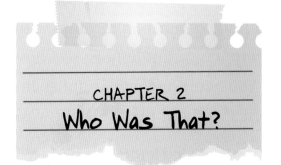

CHAPTER 2
Who Was That?

They made it to the museum on time, but only barely. When they hurried in, Amal spotted the museum's head archivist, Dr. Helga Heinfeld, leaning on the museum's front counter, as if she had been waiting for her assistant to arrive.

"I'm very sorry, Dr. Heinfeld," Amal's father said to his boss.

Dr. Heinfeld smiled, though, not mad at all. "You're right on time, Ahmed," she said. "I have a morning meeting with some very important donors, so I have to be off. You can handle your duties in the back office without my oversight, yes?"

"Of course, Dr. Heinfeld," said Dr. Farah, smiling too. "That won't be a problem at all."

"Great," said Dr. Heinfeld. She patted Amal on the head, grabbed her bag off the counter, and slipped through the museum's revolving front door.

Amal adjusted her hijab — she hated when grown-ups patted her head — and watched the doctor strut away.

"What's an important donor?" Raining Sam asked.

Dr. Farah leaned across the front counter to grab two temporary badges for the kids. "That means people who give a lot of money to the museum," he said. "Or people who donate exhibit items."

"Why does your boss have to meet with them?" Amal asked.

"It's part of her job," her father explained. "Now I have to get to my office. You two enjoy the museum. I'll meet you back here at noon for lunch."

"Okay," Amal agreed. She grabbed Raining's hand and pulled her friend deeper into the museum. "Let's start at the shuttle-missions exhibit."

"Oh, good idea," said Raining. "We can learn about Commander John Herrington."

"Was he an astronaut?" Amal asked. She knew a lot about space, and she knew the famous astronauts like everyone did, but even *she* didn't know every name from every mission. She was surprised Raining knew any of them.

"Mmhm," Raining said, nodding. They stepped through a lit archway and walked into a big room. It was still early, and the room was lit only by the display lights along the wall and around kiosks in the center of the space. "And he's a member of the Chickasaw Nation."

Amal shot him a confused look. "A member of the what?" she asked.

"He's American Indian," Raining explained. "Like me. He's just from a different tribe."

"I don't think I saw anything about him last week," Amal said. Dr. Heinfeld had given her and her father a full tour of the museum before he started.

Raining moved over to the first lighted exhibit. It showed photos of Sputnik, the Russian satellite, and the first American satellite, Explorer I.

"NASA was founded right after that," Amal said as she came to a stop next to Raining.

Raining nodded. "Herrington was like forty years later," he said. He hurried along the room, skipping past the exhibits on the Mercury Program, the Gemini Program, Apollo, and Skylab. He finally stopped five lighted kiosks over and pointed. "Here he is."

Amal hurried over to join him. On top of the kiosk, lit by a spotlight high in the ceiling, stood a model of the International Space Station. The center of the model was made up of a bunch of white tubes, and sticking off it like wings were groups of long black rectangles.

"Herrington was a mission specialist in 2002," Raining said, squinting at the backlit display on one side.

Amal circled the kiosk. It highlighted the shuttle flights to the ISS from 1998 to the present day. "Cool," she said. "So what should we do next? Maybe there's a movie we can see at the Imax or the planetarium."

Raining shrugged. "Whatever you want to do," he said.

"Wait a sec," Amal said. "I have a schedule someplace." She pulled some papers from her back pocket — brochures and flyers she'd gathered since the last time she'd put these jeans in the hamper. The papers flopped out all over the floor.

"Darn it," she said. She and Raining dropped to their knees to scoop up the paper.

"Is this it?" Raining asked. He held a glossy, two-fold brochure out to Amal.

Amal took the brochure from him and squinted at it. She couldn't see very well in the dim lighting, but she spotted a couple of familiar images: space ships and rockets and shadowy pictures of ringed planets and cratered moons. Definitely not the movie schedule.

"Oh!" she said as the answer struck her. "I totally forgot. I grabbed this from the hotel."

"Hotel?" Raining repeated.

Amal nodded. "Dad and I stayed in a hotel for two nights before we moved into our apartment," she explained. "The lobby had all kinds of brochures. This one is for a space-themed amusement park."

Raining nodded. "Oh, yeah. Francis's Flying Funland," he said. "I saw the billboard on the highway. It's only in town for a few weeks."

"We should go sometime soon," Amal suggested.

"Okay," Raining agreed. He gathered up the papers on the floor and handed the stack to Amal.

"Here it is," Amal said, spotting the schedule on top of the pile. She squinted at the movie times. "Let's find someplace with a little more light."

The two friends stood up from the dark, carpeted floor and found the nearest lighted doorway. It led to the retired space shuttle, which was on display in a huge, sunlit room. Raining whistled at the impressive ship.

"Pretty cool, huh?" Amal said. "It's the first ever reusable space ship; more than a hundred and twenty feet long."

Raining nodded with his mouth open in amazement.

"This ship here will be remembered as the grandfather of all viable space travel," Amal continued.

"Viable?" Raining repeated, sounding confused.

"It means likely to succeed," Amal said. "Anyway, let's see what movies are showing."

The two friends stood close together to look at the movie times. Just then, Amal heard the clip-clop of high-heeled shoes echoing through the chamber. From behind the massive body of the orbiter, she could just see a pair of black shoes and black slacks walk quickly and calmly through the room.

Forgetting about the movie schedule, Amal hurried over to the other side of the orbiter just in time to see whoever it was vanish into the darkness of the NASA-timeline display.

"Wasn't that your father's boss?" Raining asked, coming up next to Amal.

"I don't know," she said. "I didn't really get a good look. It must have been, though. Who else would be walking through the museum like they own the place?"

"Is it even open yet?" Raining asked.

Just then, the speaker system crackled to life, and a voice rang through the museum. "Good morning, visitors," said Jimmy, the museum's head of security. He launched into his daily announcement, the same one he made every morning, about the museum's rules and regulations.

"It's open now," Amal said. "But what would Dr. Heinfeld be doing in here? She said she had to leave."

"And we *saw* her leave," Raining
pointed out.

"Weird," Amal said. Then she shrugged.
"So, movie?"

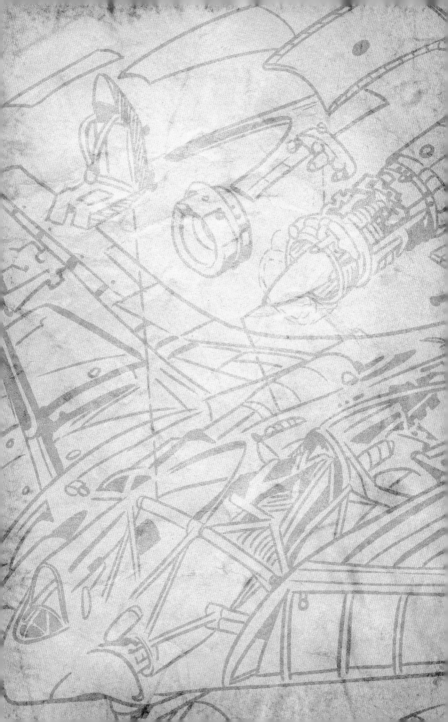

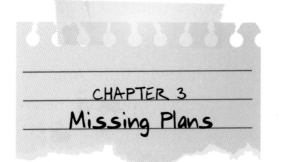

CHAPTER 3
Missing Plans

Amal and Raining caught the planetarium show about Mars, which also discussed how people could possibly travel to the red planet someday.

"Sounds impossible," Raining said as they left the theater.

"No way," Amal argued. "Nothing's impossible. We'll figure out a way."

"You're so sure?" Raining said.

Amal nodded. "I intend to go there myself someday," she said.

Raining chuckled a little. Amal would have been offended, but at the next corner she bumped right into her father.

"Oh!" Dr. Farah said, surprised. "I didn't see you." His face was flushed and he was short of breath.

"You okay?" Amal asked.

"I . . . I'm fine," her father said. "A minor office emergency. Nothing to worry about."

"Okay," Amal said. "Almost lunchtime, right?"

"Huh?" her father said. "Lunchtime? Well, enjoy!" Then he started to walk off.

"Um, Dad," Amal said, grabbing his wrist. "You're eating with me and Raining, remember?"

Her father barely seemed to hear her. "Is it raining? What a shame. Bye now." With that, he hurried off down the hallway toward the management offices.

"What do you think happened?" Raining asked.

"I don't know," Amal said. "But we better follow him."

"You think that's a good idea?" her friend asked.

"If we don't follow him, we don't eat lunch," Amal said. "What choice do we have?"

* * *

"I'm waiting for an explanation, Ahmed," a woman's voice said, sounding angry.

Amal and Raining stood just outside the door to her father's office. They would have followed him inside, but then they'd heard Dr. Heinfeld. She didn't sound happy.

"Those plans were very hard to come by," Dr. Heinfeld shouted. "I traveled to Austria and hiked through the Ötztal Alps to find a man who was 107 years old, lying on his death bed."

"I know," Dr. Farah said. "I'm —"

"And do you know what he said to me?" Dr. Heinfeld interrupted.

"No," said Dr. Farah.

"Neither do I," Dr. Heinfeld snapped. "He only spoke Friulian. I've never even *heard* of Friulian. But he sold me these plans at great cost — to our gracious donors, of course."

"Well, I'm sure that —" Dr. Farah started to say.

"How will I explain to the donors that my new assistant has lost them?" Dr. Heinfeld roared.

"But, Doctor —" said Amal's father.

But Dr. Heinfeld refused to let him get a word in. "No more excuses!" she snapped. "Find those plans or this will be your last day working at this museum!"

Angry footsteps stomped toward the door, and Amal and Raining hurried around the corner to hide.

As soon as Dr. Heinfeld's clomping footsteps were far away, Amal and Raining hurried back to Dr. Farah's office. He sat with his face down on his folded arms on his desk. "This is bad," he muttered to himself. "This is very, very bad."

"Dad?" Amal said, moving slowly closer to her father.

Dr. Farah jerked his head up quickly and faked a smile. "Amal!" he said. "How nice to see you." He started to get up. "Are you kids hungry for lunch?"

"Dad," Amal said, walking over to the desk and putting a hand on his arm. "We, um, overheard Dr. Heinfeld."

"What?" her father said, still smiling and pretending nothing was wrong. But he could tell it wasn't working. After a brief moment, he dropped back into his chair and dropped his head onto the desk again. "I don't know what to do."

"Did you really lose that thing she was talking about?" Raining asked from the doorway.

Dr. Farah shrugged. "I don't even know anymore," he said. "I did some work in the archives this morning, but I don't have any recollection of moving the Bat-Wing plans."

"Bat-Wing?" Raining said. "Like, the superhero's plane?"

Amal laughed. "No, Raining," she said. "The Bat-Wing was a super-secret German plane that was supposed to totally revolutionize flight. Some people now call it the first stealth plane. But it probably wouldn't have actually been very stealthy."

"*Wouldn't* have?" Raining said.

"It was never used," Amal explained. "A few test flights crashed, and that was that."

"And someone stole the plane?" Raining asked.

Dr. Farah shook his head. "No, no," he said. "Someone *lost* the *plans*."

"How could Dr. Heinfeld think it's your fault?" Amal said. "That's ridiculous. You never lose anything."

Amal's dad was the sort of man who liked a place for everything and everything in its place. That's why he became an archivist to begin with.

"Ridiculous or not," Dr. Farah said, "I have to find those plans. If I don't I'll lose my job."

Amal took Raining by the arm and led him into the hallway. She closed her father's office door behind them. "We need to help him," she said.

Raining nodded. "But how are we going to do that?" he asked.

"With some help from our friends," Amal said. She pulled her phone from her pocket and her thumbs flew across the keys as she typed. *My dad needs our help. Come to A&S ASAP!*

Across town, thirteen-year-old
Clementine Wim rode her silly old bicycle
as fast as it would go. The thing was
probably older than her grandmother, but
she took good care of it, and it served her
well.

Today Clementine enjoyed the midday
sun that hung over the tree-lined path

between the Capitol City Art Museum, where her mother was the Executive Assistant to the First Associate Curator of Collection Acquisitions, and the Air and Space Museum.

Clementine hadn't known Amal Farah for very long. Amal and her father had only moved to Capitol City a few weeks earlier. But Clementine was a very good judge of people, and she knew right away that she and Amal would become close friends. The fact that her two dearest friends, Raining and Wilson, had also taken so quickly to Amal confirmed that belief.

And now Amal had sent an urgent-sounding message to her and Wilson. It sounded like her father was in some kind of trouble, and she needed their help.

Clementine had immediately dropped everything — actually, she'd dropped a paintbrush she'd been using in the museum's warehouse to turn some old shipping pallets into art — and started biking.

As she pulled into the Air and Space Museum's front circle, Clementine spotted Wilson Kipper climbing out of his mother's little blue car.

"Hi, Clemmy," Wilson called. He gave her a little wave as she approached. "How's it going?"

Clementine was not a fan of nicknames, but Wilson was a good friend, so she let him get away with it. "Hi, Wilson," she said. "I guess you got Amal's message too, huh?"

Wilson nodded. "Sure did," he said. "Sounds like Amal's got a mystery to solve."

"Oh?" Clementine said. "Did you talk to her?"

"Nope," said Wilson, "but what else could it be? That's what we do, right? We solve mysteries."

* * *

A few minutes later, the four friends were gathered in the museum's cafeteria eating sandwiches and drinking sodas. Dr. Farah was so distracted by his missing-plans problem that he didn't seem to mind buying lunch for four kids instead of just two. In fact, Amal wasn't sure he'd even noticed.

After paying for their food, Dr. Farah had excused himself and gone to sit at a table alone. Amal glanced over at her father. He seemed deep in thought as he stared down at his tray, mumbling to himself and going over everything he'd done that morning.

"He's desperate," Amal said.

"We'll get to the bottom of this," Wilson said. "We need to figure out who'd want to take the plans."

"You think someone stole them?" Amal asked.

"Don't you?" said Clementine. "You must if you called us down here. It's a mystery, right?"

Amal shrugged. "It's a mystery how my dad could have lost anything," she said.

"He's beyond organized. I just can't believe it's true."

"Maybe someone else lost it," Raining said. "Who else would have been in the archives today?"

"Just Dr. Heinfeld," Amal said.

Clementine sat up straight. "Has anyone talked to Jimmy yet?" she asked. "He's head of security. Maybe he can check the security footage."

"Great idea," Amal agreed, standing up from the table. "Let's go ask him. There's no time to waste."

* * *

"No, no, no," said Jimmy, shaking his head and crossing his arms across his chest. "I can't just pull up the footage for everybody who asks."

"Does it happen a lot?" Wilson asked curiously.

"You're the second request I've had today," Jimmy told them.

"But it's possible that something was stolen," Amal said. "And my dad is being blamed!"

"Dr. Farah?" Jimmy said, actually sounding concerned. "But that's nuts. Your dad would never do anything like that."

"We know," said Wilson. "So let us see the footage, and we can prove that he didn't."

"I wish I could, kids," Jimmy said. "But the truth is, I'm not allowed to show anyone the footage without an order from the police department."

"No one?" said Amal.

"Well," said Jimmy, shifting in his chair a bit, "Dr. Heinfeld, of course. She's one of the bosses. And the board of directors could ask for anything, really. Those types of people."

"Bosses," Clementine said, and Jimmy nodded.

"Sorry, kids," said Jimmy. "I wish I could help."

Using his beefy arms and sizable belly, the security guard ushered the kids toward the door of his office and out into the hallway. Then he shut the door firmly behind them.

"Maybe we should get the police," Wilson suggested, "if that's what it takes to review the footage."

"Or we can ask the bosses, like Jimmy said," Clementine pointed out. "How about Dr. Heinfeld?"

Amal and Raining exchanged a glance. "I don't know if we should bother her," said Amal. "She was in a pretty horrible mood earlier."

"Still," Clementine said, "you heard what Jimmy said. If Dr. Heinfeld asked, he'd show her the footage. Don't you think she wants to know what happened as much as we do?"

Amal thought walking up to her dad's angry boss and asking for a favor sounded like the scariest thing she could imagine.

But what choice did she have? She had to do it for her dad.

"Okay," Amal agreed. "Let's get this over with."

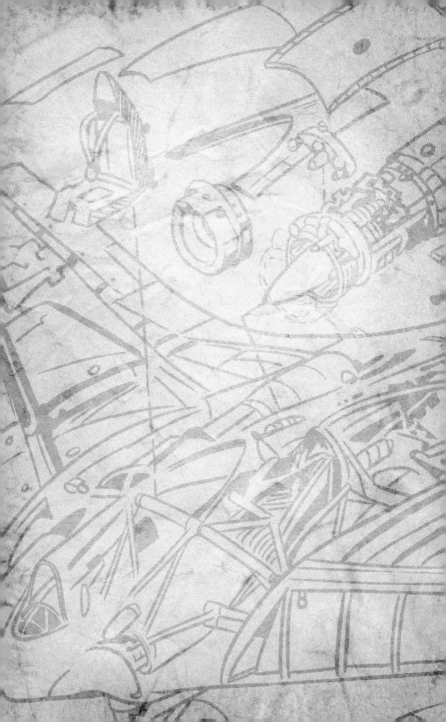

CHAPTER 5
The Usual Suspect

The four friends headed back for the management offices. They passed by museum exhibits almost without noticing: a shuttle, a lunar module, a rocket model, antique airplanes, and a huge moon landscape. One thing they passed, though, they all noticed.

"Ruthie Rothchild!" they all said together as a girl hurried past, hugging her bright red backpack.

Ruthie skidded to a stop. "Oh," she said with an irritated sigh. "It's you four. What do you want?"

They all knew Ruthie the same way they knew each other — through the network of museums in Capitol City. Ruthie's father was the Director of Temporary Exhibits at the Capitol City Museum of the Postal Service. None of them had ever been to that museum, but Ruthie showed up at their parents' museums all the time.

"We don't want anything," Amal said, stepping up to the other girl. They were the same age, and Amal knew Ruthie would probably be in some of her classes in the fall. She wasn't looking forward to it.

"What are you doing here, anyway?" Amal continued. "You're not supposed to have your bag inside the museum. You should have checked it at the front desk when you came in."

"I'm going there *now*," Ruthie snapped. "So there." Then she hurried off, apparently toward the bag check.

"She's up to something," said Wilson skeptically as they watched Ruthie hurry away from them.

"She's always up to something," Clementine agreed.

The four stood there a moment, thinking it over, and then hurried on to Dr. Heinfeld's office.

"She's not here," Amal said, peering through the narrow window of Dr. Heinfeld's office. It was dark inside. "I wonder where she went."

"It doesn't matter," Clementine said with a shrug. "We don't need her anymore anyway."

"We don't?" Wilson said, sounding confused. "Why not?"

Clementine shook her head. "Because," she said, "Ruthie did it. Isn't that obvious?"

Clementine might not have had a good reason to suspect Ruthie — other than their history. Of the four friends, Clementine had known Ruthie the longest.

Even though Ruthie was a couple years younger, she and Clementine had grown up together — and Ruthie had always been bigger and meaner.

When they were four and six, Clementine had invited Ruthie to paint with her. Ruthie thanked her by dumping a whole bottle of paint on Clementine's artwork.

When they were nine and eleven, Clementine had invited Ruthie to her birthday party. Ruthie came and knocked the cake off the table — and right onto Clementine, who just so happened to be wearing her favorite dress.

"Oops," Ruthie had said, pretending it was an accident. Their parents had believed her. Clementine had not.

And just a few weeks ago, Clementine had finished her final project for her sculpture class. She'd loved it . . . until Ruthie came along. The younger girl had balled up her hand into a mean little fist and punched Clementine's copy of Rodin's *Thinker* right in the face. The still-soft clay had smooshed, and after that, Clementine's project didn't look much like a thinker anymore.

"Clemmy," said Wilson, "are you sure you're not just assuming the worst about Ruthie because . . . well . . ."

"Because she *is* the worst?" Amal finished for him.

"Yes, she *is* the worst," Clementine agreed. "But she also had a bag. We should search it."

"We can't just go around searching people's bags," Amal said.

"Not *people*," Clementine argued. Her voice was quiet, but still a little angry. "Just Ruthie."

Amal smiled and put an arm around her friend. "If she stole the plans," she said, "we'll find the clues to prove it. I promise."

CHAPTER 6
New Leads

The four friends tracked Ruthie down
again in the cafeteria. She was sitting at
a table alone, but this time, her bag was
nowhere to be seen.

"I'll handle this," Amal said. Since it
was her father in danger of losing his job,
she might as well be the one doing the
questioning.

Amal marched straight over to the other girl, pulled out an empty chair, and plopped down at the table. "So, Ruthie," she said, "care to tell me where you were this morning between nine and lunchtime?"

Ruthie glared at Amal and then scooted her chair further away. "That," she said, snarling, "is absolutely none of your business."

"It sounds to me like you're trying to hide something," Amal said. "Like maybe you were snooping around in the archives!"

Ruthie sneered. "Oh, please," she said. "Why would I waste my time hanging out there? I don't even know where the stupid old archives are."

"Ha!" Amal said. "A likely excuse."

Ruthie just rolled her eyes. "Stop acting like you're the police or something," she said. "I can do what I want, and you can't stop me."

"Oh, yeah?" Amal said.

"Yeah," Ruthie said. "And now I want to leave." With that she pushed her chair back and stepped around Amal. She stuck her tongue out at the others and stomped out of the cafeteria.

Wilson ran over to Amal. "I think you spooked her," he said.

Amal shook her head. "That was a waste of time. We're not going to get anything out of her," she said. "We need some new leads."

"Let's talk to Jimmy again," said Raining Sam. "I know it sounds weird, but think about it. He had the opportunity. He's always in the museum from open to close."

"True," said Amal, "but so were you and I *and* my dad."

"But Jimmy also had the means," Raining said. "Since he controls the cameras, he could have made sure they were off. Or he could have erased the video to cover his tracks."

"That is a good point," Clementine agreed.

"But why would he do it?" Wilson asked. "Ruthie might do it just because she doesn't like Amal, and she wants her dad to get fired."

"Didn't Dr. Heinfeld say the plans are really expensive?" said Raining. "I bet Jimmy could use a little extra spending money."

"He does have new twins at home," Amal said. "It was one of the first things he told me when I met him last week. Let's go talk to him."

Amal started walking fast out of the cafeteria toward Jimmy's security office, but Clementine grabbed her arm and stopped her.

"Um," Clementine said, "maybe you should let one of us handle it this time. We don't want Jimmy running off like Ruthie did."

* * *

On the way back to Jimmy's security office, the four friends crossed through the front lobby. In the center of the room, standing near the wide, gleaming white front desk, they spotted Dr. Heinfeld. She wasn't alone.

Standing beside the head archivist was a man with a long, lean face and thin, black hair combed straight back from his forehead. He was quite a bit taller than Dr. Heinfeld, but a little bit hunched over, and he wasn't dressed like the people she usually talked to. Most of them wore nice suits. This man had on jeans and a denim shirt. His hands were dirty, like he'd just been working on a car.

"Who is that man?" Clementine asked, looking curious.

Amal shook her head. "I don't know," she replied. "I've never seen him here before. I don't think he works at the museum."

Raining took a step toward the pair, but Amal grabbed his shirt. "Where are you going?" she asked.

Raining frowned and took another step forward. "That man looks so familiar," he said, still focused on the pair of adults. "I'm sure I've seen him before." Then he took another step.

"Raining," Amal snapped. "Come back here."

But her friend ignored her. Raining quickly crossed the lobby and walked straight up to Dr. Heinfeld and the stranger. He stood right beside them, staring at the man's face. The grownups didn't seem to notice him.

"Excuse me," Raining finally said. The adults immediately stopped their hushed conversation and glanced down at Raining.

"Who are you?" Dr. Heinfeld asked, seeming irritated at the interruption. "Oh, you're Dr. Farah's kid's friend. What do you want?"

"I was wondering," said Raining, looking at the man, "do I know you from somewhere?"

The man shook his head. "I don't think so, kid," he said with a nervous smile.

"I'm sure I've seen your face before," Raining insisted.

"Well," the man replied, "my face does show up here and there. You might have seen it. But I don't think we've met before. Sorry, kid. "

Dr. Heinfeld shot Raining another irritated look. "Why don't we go talk someplace a little more private?" she suggested, leading the man out of the lobby.

Amal, Clementine, and Wilson hurried over to Raining. "Well?" said Amal. "What did they say to you?"

"Not much," said Raining. "But that man is up to no good."

"Why do you say that?" Clementine asked curiously.

"His smile," said Raining. "Something's not right about that guy." He tapped his chin with his finger. "I can't quite put my finger on it, but I know I've seen him someplace before. I just know it."

CHAPTER 7
Bag Check

Jimmy sat in his office talking to a photo of two pudgy babies when Amal and her friends walked back in.

"I'll be home in a few hours, my little ginger snaps!" the security guard cooed at the picture.

"Hi, Jimmy," Amal said, snapping him out of his daydream.

"Amal!" Jimmy said, grabbing onto the armrests of his chair and sending the photo of his kids gliding to the desk. "What are you doing back here? I already told you I can't show that footage to anyone."

Amal opened her mouth to speak, but Clementine stepped in front of her. "I'll handle this," she said quietly. Then she grinned at Jimmy. He grinned back.

"Hey, Jimmy," Clementine said in her sweetest voice. "Congratulations on your new babies."

"Thank you, Clementine," he said. "That's very nice of you. I'm so proud of my baby girls."

"Maybe I can babysit for you someday," Clementine offered.

"Oh, I don't know," said Jimmy. "I'm not sure my wife will ever let those two out of her sight. She's pretty protective of our little girls."

"Of course," said Clementine. "So, Jimmy. I was wondering. Do you stay here in your security office all day?"

"Yep," Jimmy said. "All day."

"Don't you leave for lunch?" Clementine asked, sitting on the edge of his desk. She picked up the photo of his twins and studied it.

"Well," said Jimmy, snatching the photo from her, "of course I do."

"Oh, so you *do* leave sometimes," said Clementine. "For lunch or for coffee maybe?"

"I guess," Jimmy said, shrugging. "If I need an afternoon snack."

"Of course," said Clementine.

"I get a little hungry around two-thirty," Jimmy admitted.

"Me too," said Clementine. "In fact, it's almost two-thirty now. Maybe I can grab something for you in the cafeteria?"

"That'd be nice of you," Jimmy said. He leaned a little closer and whispered, "See if they have any chocolate-glazed doughnuts."

Clementine grinned and hopped down from the desk. "You got it. Oh, one more thing, before I go," she added. "Did you leave the security office this morning at all, like between opening and lunchtime?"

"Hmm," said Jimmy, furrowing his brow. Then he snapped his fingers. "I did! I took a walk to the vending machines on the second floor."

"The ones with Choco-Peanut-Goober bars," said Clementine, nodding.

Jimmy smiled. "You got it," he said.

"And you bought a bar?" she asked.

"Two," Jimmy confessed, blushing a little bit.

Clementine looked around the room for a garbage can. She spotted one in the corner and shot a glance at Wilson. He nodded and hurried over to the trashcan. Reaching in, he pulled out two bright red-and-yellow wrappers, their insides stained with chocolate, and held them up.

"Okay, Jimmy," said Clementine. "I'll drop by with a doughnut for you a little later. Bye!"

As they left Jimmy's office, Clementine shrugged. "His story checks out," she said. "He went and bought some candy."

"But that doesn't mean it's *all* he did," Wilson pointed out. "He had the opportunity to grab the plans, too."

"I guess," Clementine admitted. "I think he's clean."

The four friends came to a stop behind the museum's front desk. The ticket taker was on the phone at the far end. Right in front of them were a dozen cubbyholes, some with bags in them.

Amal elbowed Clementine gently. "Recognize any of those?" she asked.

Clementine scanned the collection of checked bags. One of them, bright red with a green tag and purple drawings on it, was familiar. "Ruthie's!" she declared.

Amal nodded.

Clementine opened her eyes wide. "Should we?" she said. "It doesn't seem right."

The ticket taker was paying no attention to the four kids standing nearby.

"We have to," Amal said. "We have to solve this crime."

"We don't even know if it *is* a crime," Raining pointed out.

"It must be," Amal said. Before anyone could stop her, she darted behind the desk and grabbed Ruthie's bag. Then she slung it over her shoulder and hurried off. Her friends followed till they were safely out of sight, sitting in the shadow of the lunar module.

Amal unzipped the bag and dumped the contents onto the floor. There were books and a hand-held video game and a makeup bag and brochures and flyers from every museum in the city.

"Wow," Amal said. "Why does she need so much *stuff*?"

The kids spread everything out, hoping to find something that looked like Bat-Wing plans. But nothing did.

"This looks familiar," said Raining. He grabbed a glossy brochure and held it up for them to see. "You have the same one in your pocket."

"Oh, yeah," said Amal. "Flying Funland."

Raining flipped it over. "I've got it," he said. He pointed at a little picture on the back. It was a man's face.

"Him?" Amal asked. She shrugged. "Who is he?"

"That's Francis," said Clementine, craning her neck to read the photo's caption. "As in Francis's Flying Funland."

Raining nodded. "*And* he's the man your dad's boss was talking to in the lobby!"

"What's he doing here?" Amal said.

Raining scanned the brochure. All the rides at the amusement park were based on spaceships and airplanes from over the decades. Some looked like brand-new shuttles, and some looked like antique flying machines. "He doesn't have the Bat-Wing," Raining pointed out.

"So?" said Amal.

"So maybe he'd like to," said Clementine. "And he needs the plans to make one."

Amal and Wilson nodded. The four sleuths were on to something.

"Now all we have to do is track down this Francis guy and prove our theory," said Amal.

Just then, a familiar voice echoed through the room. "I'll be ready in a minute, Mom!" a girl called. "I have to get my bag from the front desk!"

"Ruthie!" the friends exclaimed together.

As quickly as they could, the four of them crammed everything back inside Ruthie's bag. Then they ran over to the front desk.

In the lobby they saw Ruthie — heading straight for the bag-check counter. She was between them and the desk. They'd have to get past her without letting her see that *they* had her bag.

Amal quickly passed the bag to Raining, who hurried to the edge of the lobby. Clementine called out, "Hey, Ruthie!"

The other girl spun around and sneered at Clementine. "What do *you* want?" she snapped.

"Um . . ." said Clementine. She tried to keep her eyes off Raining as he snuck around the lobby toward the front desk. "I was just wondering . . . if you . . . um . . . had a nice time at the museum today. Was it fun?"

Ruthie rolled her eyes. "You're being even weirder than you usually are," she said, turning back around.

Before Ruthie could bust Raining, Amal ran over and stood in front of her. "Hi, Ruthie," she said, blocking the other girl's path and view of the desk. She frantically waved to Clementine to hurry up around them.

Clementine ran past them.

"Did you see the, um, space shuttle?" Amal asked.

"Obviously," said Ruthie. She went to step past, but Amal blocked her again. "Would you move?!"

"How about the Martian skeleton?" Amal asked.

"The what?" said Ruthie. "There's no Martian skeleton here . . . is there?"

Meanwhile, Clementine grabbed Ruthie's bag from Raining and hurried to the front desk. But the ticket taker was off the phone now, and she was watching the whole scene very closely.

"Hello," Clementine said sweetly.

"Hello," said the ticket taker, trying not to smile.

"I'd like to check this bag, please," Clementine said.

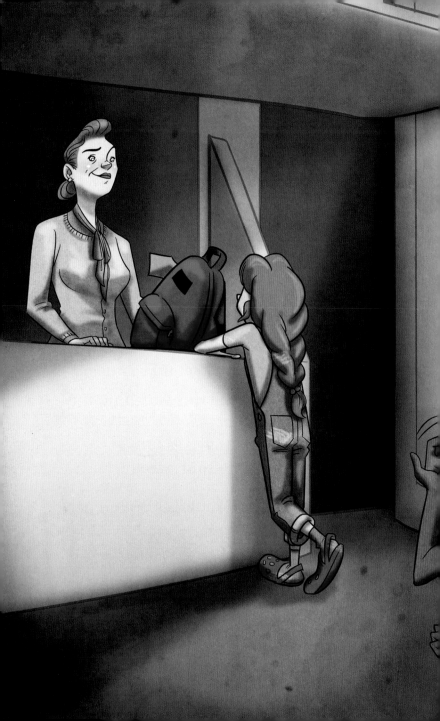

"*Your* bag?" the ticket taker asked.

"Um . . ." Clementine said, "something like that."

"I see," said the ticket taker. "How about I just slip it back into this cubby? The same one it was in when your *friend* dropped it off a couple of hours ago?"

"Ha!" said Clementine. "Sounds good to me." She checked over her shoulder. Amal had done a great job slowing her down, but now Ruthie was heading her way.

"Oh, gotta go!" said Clementine as she hurried away. "Thanks!"

She joined her friends and watched as Ruthie went up to the counter. The girl glared at Amal, Clementine, Wilson, and Raining, but she didn't seem to know what they'd done.

"My bag, please," said Ruthie. "It's bright red with a green tag."

"Oh, I know just the one," said the ticket taker.

The four friends sighed with relief as they pushed through the museum's front door. As soon as they were outside, they busted up laughing.

"Wow," said Amal. "*That* was close."

"*Too* close," said Clementine.

"But it was worth it," said Raining, "even if she didn't take the plans."

"Right," said Amal. "Because now we know who *did*."

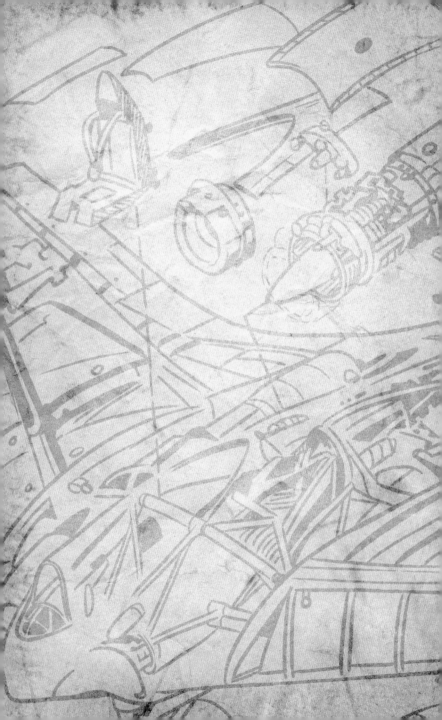

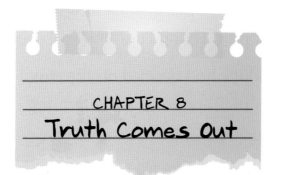

CHAPTER 8
Truth Comes Out

"Dr. Heinfeld?" Amal said, sticking her head into the boss's office. "I'm sorry to bother you, but do you have a minute to talk?"

The doctor sighed at the four kids standing in her doorway. "I really don't," she said.

"It's really important," said Amal. "Do you know how we can get in touch with Francis from Flying Funland?"

The kids had decided on the way to Dr. Heinfeld's office not to say anything about their suspicions, just in case they were wrong.

"How would I know?" Dr. Heinfeld asked angrily.

"Weren't you talking to him in the lobby earlier?" Amal asked. "We saw you with him."

"The man in jeans," Raining added. "He kind of looked like an auto mechanic."

Dr. Heinfeld stood up and paced behind her desk. "Oh, that man," she said. "I didn't know his name." She shrugged and then sat down. "He was just a museum visitor asking about some display."

"Oh," said Amal. "It looked like you knew him."

"Well, I didn't," said Dr. Heinfeld. With that, she closed the door in their faces.

"Well, that was rude," Amal muttered under her breath.

"Now what do we do?" said Wilson. "Can we go to Flying Funland to find him?"

"Now," said Clementine, "it's doughnut time."

"What?" said Amal. "You're hungry?"

"No," said Clementine, "but I promised Jimmy."

"There were two chocolate-glazed doughnuts left," Clementine said when they walked back into the security office. "I bought both, just in case."

"Oh, thank you," Jimmy said gratefully. He grabbed the paper sack and peered inside, licking his lips eagerly. "I'm sure glad you showed up when you did. Normally I'd have my snack from home for the afternoon."

"Forgot it today?" Clementine asked.

Jimmy took an enormous bite from a doughnut — big enough that it was half gone afterward. "Nope," he said. "I never forget a snack. But this morning Dr. Heinfeld came by — I mentioned that, didn't I?"

"I don't think so," Clementine said, glancing at her friends gathered near the security office door.

Jimmy finished the first doughnut. "No big deal," he said. "She was here. She said she forgot to eat breakfast and took my extra banana muffin."

"So she just took it?" Clementine said. "How rude."

"Well, she *is* the boss," Jimmy replied with a shrug.

"True," said Clementine. "Does she drop by to steal muffins a lot?"

Jimmy shook his head. "No," he said. "But she wasn't here just for the muffin. She wanted to check out some security footage first."

"Why?" Clementine asked, sensing she was onto something. Her friends moved closer to the desk.

"Who knows?" said Jimmy, shrugging. "Like I said, she's the boss."

"Well, what footage did she watch?" Clementine asked.

"A few minutes from the archives camera, I think," said Jimmy.

"What was on the footage?" asked Amal, leaning closer.

"I don't know," said Jimmy. He grabbed the second doughnut. "She asked me to take a walk while she watched. That's when I got my candy bars."

"I see," Clementine said thoughtfully. "Enjoy your doughnuts."

"Thanks," said Jimmy, his mouth full and the doughnuts gone.

Clementine and her friends hurried from the office. "That's all the evidence I need," she said.

Amal nodded. "Should I tell my dad?" she asked. "He'll be so relieved."

"We'd better prove it first," Wilson pointed out.

Raining nodded. "I think Francis will have the proof," he said.

"We still have to find him," Wilson pointed out.

"And we don't have long to do it," said Amal. "The museum will close soon, and if those plans aren't back by the end of the day, my dad will lose his job."

Wilson checked the watch he wore on his wrist — it had a picture of a Pterosaur on it. Nearly everything he owned had a picture of a Pterosaur on it. "My mom will be here soon to pick me up," he said.

"That's perfect," said Amal. "So you think she can give us all a ride someplace?"

* * *

Dr. Kipper was happy to drive the four of them anywhere, especially if it meant helping Dr. Farah. In no time at all they pulled up to Francis's Flying Funland, and the four sleuths piled out.

From the parking lot they could see huge models of the planets with an exciting roller coaster ride zooming around each one. There were spinning plane rides and bouncing lunar module rides.

"Wow," said Amal. It was amazing.

"I'll wait right here," Dr. Kipper called after them. "Don't be too long, please."

They ran to the front gate. "Excuse me," Wilson said to the ticket taker. "We need to speak to Francis right away. It's an emergency."

"Sorry," said the ticket taker. "I can't let you in without a ticket."

"How much?" Clementine asked.

"For four of you?" said the ticket taker. "That'll come out to two hundred and forty dollars."

"We don't have that kind of money!" Amal exclaimed.

"Sorry," said the ticket taker. "No money, no tickets."

Just then, a pickup truck screeched to a stop in a nearby parking space marked "Reserved." The man they'd seen at the museum earlier climbed out carrying a manila folder under his arm.

"Francis!" Raining shouted, running over to him.

"You again," said the man. "Why do you keep bugging me?"

"We don't mean to bug you," Amal said as the other three ran up to the man as well. "But we're trying to help my dad. He's in a lot of trouble."

"I'm sorry to hear that," said Francis, "but I don't see how I can help you."

"He's in trouble," said Clementine. "And I'm guessing it's because of that file under your arm."

Looking surprised, Francis pulled out the file and opened it. "I don't understand," he said. "I bought these from a very stern woman at the Air and Space Museum."

"That's what we figured," said Amal. "But she wasn't supposed to sell them. They belong in the archives at the Air and Space Museum."

"And now she's blaming Amal's father for them being missing," said Raining.

"He's going to lose his job," Amal said.

"I see," said Francis. "We'd better get back to the museum and get this straightened out right away."

Dr. Kipper stuck her head out the driver's side window. "Kids," she called, "we should get going. The museum will close soon."

"I'll follow your car," said Francis. "Let's hurry."

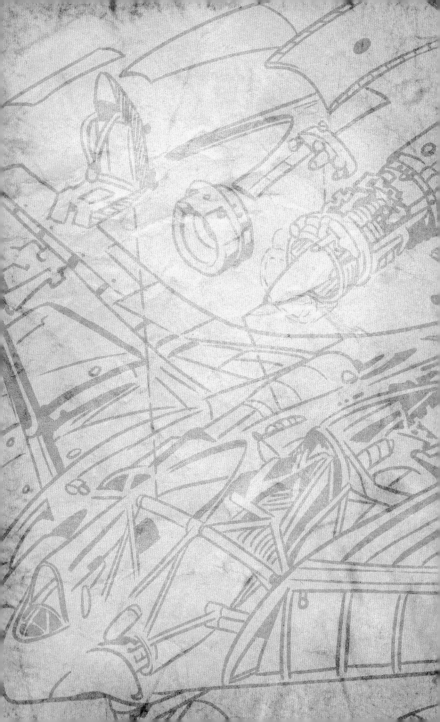

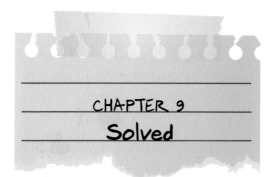

CHAPTER 9
Solved

Dr. Heinfeld and Dr. Farah were both in the lobby when the kids got back to the museum. Dr. Farah was frowning and holding a box filled with all the personal items from his office.

With them stood a tall elderly man wearing a very nice suit. He had a bushy white mustache and crazy white hair, and he was shaking his head sadly.

"That's Mr. Janovic," said Amal quietly. "He's the chairman."

"I'm afraid I see no other option, Dr. Farah," said Mr. Janovic. "I have no choice but to fire you."

"Sir," said Dr. Farah. "If you'll just —"

"Not another word out of you," said Dr. Heinfeld, cutting him off. She grabbed Dr. Farah's elbow and started pulling him toward the door, but the four friends blocked her way.

"Excuse me!" the head archivist said. "Move aside."

"I don't think so," Clementine said, crossing her arms in front of her chest.

"Sir," Amal said to Mr. Janovic, "you're firing the wrong person."

"Is that so?" the chairmain said. "And whom should I be firing?"

"Ask Francis," Amal said. She stepped aside, and Francis walked up to the chairman.

"Sir," Francis said, "I'm afraid I'm involved in this." He handed over the manila folder.

Mr. Janovic, a bewildered look on his face, opened it up. "Oh my goodness!" he said. "The missing plans! Where did you get these?"

Dr. Heinfeld ran over and grabbed the plans out of his hands. "How dare you!" she snapped at Francis. "You stole these from the museum when you were here earlier, didn't you?"

"She's lying!" Wilson exclaimed.

"She's the one who stole them," said Raining.

"And she erased the video in the security office," Clementine added, glaring in Dr. Heinfeld's direction.

"And she framed my dad," said Amal, "and sold the plans to Francis for his park."

Francis nodded. "I'm afraid that's right," he said regretfully. "If I'd known they were stolen, I never would have bought them."

"I see," said Mr. Janovic. "Is this true, Dr. Heinfeld?"

"Of course not!" she said. "It's totally ridiculous."

"I will get to the bottom of this," Mr. Janovic said. "Meanwhile, Dr. Farah. You're *un*fired."

"Thank you, sir," said Dr. Farah. Leaning down, he kissed his daughter on the cheek. With a grateful smile, he hurried away to unpack.

Just then, Jimmy came out of the security office. "We're about to close, folks," he said. "Oh, Dr. Heinfeld. Did you enjoy that banana muffin?"

"What banana muffin?" Mr. Janovic asked.

"The doctor had one of my muffins," Jimmy explained, "when she stopped by this morning to go over the security video footage."

"So you *did* erase the video!" said Mr. Janovic. He held Dr. Heinfeld in place with an even, icy stare. "*You* are fired, Dr. Heinfeld."

Dr. Heinfeld's mouth dropped open in shock. "You can't be serious! You're not taking the word of four children and one security guard over *mine*, are you?" she said, aghast.

"I most certainly am," Mr. Janovic said. "Clean out your office — now. Our *new* head archivist, Dr. Farah, will be needing it."

With that, the chairman strode away, and Amal, Clementine, Wilson, and Raining cheered.

Dr. Heinfeld, however, was furious. She stomped her high-heeled shoe on the ground so hard that the heel broke. When she tried to storm out of the lobby, her uneven walk, on just one heel, had everyone laughing.

"Another mystery solved," said Wilson proudly.

"And we got it done before closing time," Clementine added.

"Tomorrow you kids should come down to Flying Funland," Francis said.

"We'd love to," Amal said. "But we can't afford those tickets. The museums are free for us."

"Don't worry about the price," said Francis. "You know the owner!"

Steve B.

About the Author

Steve Brezenoff is the author of more than fifty middle-grade chapter books, including the Field Trip Mysteries series, the Ravens Pass series of thrillers, and the Return to Titanic series. In his spare time, he enjoys video games, cycling, and cooking. Steve lives in Minneapolis with his wife, Beth, and their son and daughter.

Lisa W.

About the Illustrator

Lisa K. Weber is an illustrator currently living in Oakland, California. She graduated from Parsons School of Design in 2000 and then began freelancing. Since then, she has completed many print, animation, and design projects, including graphic novelizations of classic literature, character and background designs for children's cartoons, and textiles for dog clothing.

 GLOSSARY

astronaut (ASS-truh-nawt) — someone who travels in space

astronomy (uh-STRON-uh-mee) — the study of stars, planets, and space

brochure (broh-SHUR) — a booklet, usually with pictures, that gives information about a product or service

donor (DOH-nur) — someone who gives something, usually to an organization or a charity

exhibit (eg-ZIB-it) — to show something in public

gracious (GRAY-shuhss) — very polite in a way that shows respect

planetarium (plan-uh-TAIR-ee-uhm) — a building with equipment for reproducing the positions and movements of the sun, moon, planets, and stars by projecting their images onto a curved ceiling

stealthy (STEL-thee) — secret and quiet

viable (VYE-uh-buhl) — workable or capable of succeeding

DISCUSSION QUESTIONS

1. Do you think it was fair for Amal and her friends to immediately suspect Ruthie? Talk about why or why not.

2. Were you surprised to find out who the real culprit was? Talk about who else you might have suspected if you were on the case.

3. Would you ever want to travel into space? Why or why not? Discuss the reasons behind your decision.

WRITING PROMPTS

1. Write a chapter that continues this book. What happens after the kids solve the mystery of the missing plans?

2. There are several museums in the Capitol City network. Write a paragraph about which one you think would be most interesting to visit and why.

3. Amal and her friends each have their own interests and hobbies. Write a paragraph about one of your hobbies or interests. What do you enjoy about it?

AIR AND SPACE INFORMATION

The National Air and Space Museum, which opened in Washington D.C. in 1976, is one of the country's most popular museums. The museum welcomes more than eight million visitors each year and is dedicated to educating the public about the history of aviation and astronomy.

Space Exploration:

NASA is an acronym that stands for National Aeronautics and Space Administration.

NASA became operational on October 1, 1958 — one year after the Soviets launched Sputnik 1, the world's first artificial satellite.

The International Space Station is the largest artificial body in orbit and is approximately the same length and width as a football field. It is so large, in fact, that it can often be seen from Earth without a telescope.

Aviation Facts:

The Wright brothers, Orville and Wilbur, are credited with inventing and building the world's first successful airplane and making the first controlled, sustained human flight on December 17, 1903.

The **Wright 1905 Flyer**, the first practical airplane, flew for 33 minutes and 17 seconds, covering a distance of twenty miles, on October 4, 1905.

Ready for more MYSTERY?

MUSEUM MYSTERIES

Check out the Capitol City sleuths'
next adventure and help them solve
crime in some of the city's
most important museums!

The Capitol City Natural
History Museum is
haunted — or at least that's
what someone wants people
to think. But Wilson Kipper,
son of the museum's head
paleontologist, knows better.
When the strange occurrences
start to turn dangerous, the
museum is forced to close
its doors. Can Wilson and his
friends get to the bottom
of things, or will the Natural
History Museum be shut
down for good?